CAN DO IT,
NOISY NORA!

‹ R O S E M A R Y   W E L L S ›

VIKING

VIKING
An imprint of Penguin Random House LLC, New York

First published in the United States of America
by Viking, an imprint of Penguin Random House LLC, 2020

Visit us online at penguinrandomhouse.com

LIBRARY OF CONGRESS CATALOGING-IN-PUBLICATION DATA IS AVAILABLE.
ISBN 9781101999233

Manufactured in China

The art for this book was done in watercolors on Saunders cold press linen paper.

1 3 5 7 9 10 8 6 4 2

Petra Beezoo Frances Phoebe Lexie

For my string septet

Ellie Zoey

From a neighbor's window,
on a night in June,

Nora heard a violin
playing *Clair de lune*.
The music floated like a cloud,

dreamy, soft, and true.
Nora wished with all her heart
that she could play it too.

"How about the xylophone?"
said Father with a smile.

"Or the banjo," Mama added,
"would surely be worthwhile."

"Anything," yelled sister Kate,
"except a screeching violin!"

But Nora wanted what she wanted,
and she dug her heels in.

Mrs. Yamamoto
brought the violin.

"There's much to learn and practice
before we can begin.

"First things first," she said.
"Here's the way we hold the bow.
Standing firmly on both legs,
press the strings . . . just so!

"*Twinkle, Twinkle, Little Star*
will be our starter tune,"
said Mrs. Yamamoto.
"You'll learn it very soon!"

MONDAY

TWANG!

TUESDAY

WHINE!

FRIDAY

SCREECH!

SATURDAY

PLUCK!

WEDNESDAY

SCRAPE!

THURSDAY

SQUEAK!

SUNDAY

SHRIEK!

was Nora's music for a week.

Twinkle, Twinkle, Little Star
came squealing through the breeze.

"Nora," yelled sister Kate.
"Close your door, please!"

Practice hours felt like years.
Everybody held their ears.
"Awful!" squawked the cockatoo.
Jack woke up and cried.

"Brava!" said her mama.
"But let's play again outside!"

Sawing like a buzz saw,
scratching like a hen,
with Father for conductor,
Nora tried again.

Kate put on her earmuffs.
Jack began to howl.
The cockatoo was covered
with a heavy bathroom towel.

September 1st was going to be
a very special day.
Nora had a brand-new song
she wanted so to play.

"You can do it!" said her teacher.
And in a monumental burst,
Nora learned it perfectly
on August 31st.

The special evening came at last!

Not a sound was heard!

No "tra la la" from Jack,
no comments from the bird.

Safely underneath her chin,
Nora tucked her violin.

Happy Birthday, Mama!
Across the yard it rang.
Every note played true and strong.

And everybody sang!